Penny Dreadful
Becomes a Bridesmaid
page 97

Meet Penny Dreadful and her Resigned Relations...

Penny
(It's never really her fault...)

Cosmo
(Penny's best friend)

Georgia May Morton-Jones
(Penny's genius cousin)

Daisy
(Penny's annoying sister)

Penny's long-suffering **mom** and **dad**

Very prim-and-proper
Aunt Deedee

Barry
(Meow, I'm Gran's cat)

Gran
(Normally found fast asleep somewhere)

...her Crazy Classmates, and Sick and Tired Teachers

Bridget Grimes (Star student)

Mr. Schumann (**SICK AND TIRED** principal)

Henry Potts (Cosmo's mortal enemy)

Sandwich fan, **Alexander Pringle**

Miss Patterson (Penny's tall-and-thin-like-a-beanpole teacher)

Shaves-his-head-every-week **Brady O'Grady**

Cherry Scarpelli (Bridget's best-friend-forever)

Luke Bruce (Puts things up his nose)

Penny Dreadful

and the Horrible Hoopla

By Joanna Nadin

Illustrated by Jess Mikhail

Contents

My name is not actually Penny Dreadful. It is Penelope Jones. The "Dreadful" part is my dad's **JOKE**. I know it is a joke because every time he says it he laughs like a honking goose.

But I do not see the funny side. Plus it is not even true that I am dreadful. It is like Gran says, i.e. that I am a **MAGNET FOR DISASTER**. Mom says if Gran kept a better eye on me in the first place instead of on *Divas Dish* on TMI network then I might not be quite so magnetic. But Gran says if Mom wasn't so busy answering phones for Dr. Cement, who is her boss, and who has bulgy eyes like hard-boiled eggs (which is why everyone calls him Dr. Bugeye), and Dad wasn't so busy solving crises at the city council, then they would be able to solve some crises at 73 Rollins Road, i.e. our house. So you see it is completely not my fault.

★ ☆ ✦ ✦

Sometimes it is the fault of my sister Daisy, who is very **IRRITATING**. And who is especially irritating when she is trying to be a rock star with her best friend Lucy B. Finnegan, because they are mostly arguing over who is going to be the lead singer and who is going to do backup with swaying hips and doo-wops, e.g. going "*I am,*" "*No I am,*" "*No I am.*" So it is not my fault if I borrow the microphone while they are arguing to see if it works underwater and it does not.

And sometimes it is the fault of Cosmo Moon Webster, who is my best friend even though he is a week older than me and a boy. Because if it wasn't for his mom Sunflower (whose real name is Barbara) being so **BIG** on **FREEDOM** and **SELF-EXPRESSION**, then we would not have been **FREE** to paint ourselves purple and pretend to be minions of Maximus Terror, leader of the Zombiebots. And then Mrs. Butterworth (who works at the general store and has a mustache and a beady eye, which is mostly on me) would not have had the **HEEBIE-JEEBIES** and had to go to see Dr. Cement for some medicine to recover.

And sometimes it is the fault of Dad, because he is mostly saying, e.g. *"I could have been an escapologist if I hadn't met your mom,"* only Mom says he could not because he cannot even find his way down a one-way street, let alone a locked cage. And it turns out she is right because when I lock him in the bathroom he completely cannot get the door open and has to come out of the window in only a towel, which gives Mrs. Butterworth the **HEEBIE-JEEBIES** again and so it is back to Dr. Cement.

But this week it is the fault of someone else completely and that is Hilary O. Henderson, and also maybe Mom, who should have said:

a) No dressing as **HOOLIGANS**.

2. No dipping things in **HONEY** and **SPRINKLES**.

iii) No using **MYSTERIOUS MONKEY HANDS**.

What happens is that normally I am not **BIG** on babysitters because they are mostly old people with beady eyes and mustaches, like e.g. Mrs. Butterworth, who say no you **CANNOT** eat fourteen cookies and then jump up and down on the sofa to see how long it is before you are sick, you can **SIT STILL** and read a book about otters.

And Mom is not big on babysitters either because they are mostly old people with beady eyes and mustaches, like e.g. Mrs. Butterworth, who say, "In my day children knew the **MEANING** of the word **DISCIPLINE**." And Mom says **I DO** know the meaning, but she tests me and I do not, unless **DISCIPLINE** is a sort of a dinosaur. Which is

why it is either Gran who is left in charge, or if
it is bingo night then no one goes out, because it
is **NOT WORTH THE HOOPLA**.

But on Saturday something **UNPREDICTABLE**
happens which means no one knew it was coming
(which I know because Miss Patterson, who is our
teacher and who is tall and thin like a beanpole,
said it was completely **UNPREDICTABLE** when
the eraser I was throwing at Henry Potts, who
is Cosmo's mortal enemy, pinged off a poster
about potatoes and hit our principal Mr.
Schumann on the ear just as he was coming
into our class to tell us we had won Class of the
Week for being excellent – only he changed his
mind and it went to 3C who made a collage
about cows, and I got a gold star taken away,

which I said was unfair but Mom said was completely **PREDICTABLE**).

But this **UNPREDICTABLE** thing is even more **DISASTROUS** because it is that Mom and Dad have got to go to the Traffic Circle Ball and they cannot say no because Mr. Hobnob, who is Dad's boss and who has hair like a hedgehog, will **FROWN** on them,

and he is already **FROWNING** on Dad for several things, i.e.:

1. Moving some traffic cones from one side of the road (which was the left side of the road) to the right side of the road (which was the **WRONG** side of the road).

b) Building a tower with a hole punch, a stapler and a machine-that-goes-beep, which collapsed and the machine-that-goes-beep knocked over a cup of coffee that went spill, and it was all over an important picture of a parking meter.

3. Going to a crucial meeting about crosswalks in a helmet made of a flowerpot and a remote-control car, which was not completely my fault, it was a **PATENT BRAIN MASSAGING HELMET**, only it was too small for Dad's enormous brain and got stuck.

And Gran has to go dancing with her friend Arthur Peason and she cannot say no because Arthur will **FROWN** on her, and he is already **FROWNING** on her for several things, i.e.:

a) Beating him at Texas Hold 'Em seventeen times,  which she says was because of beginner's luck but Arthur says was down to the ace of spades in her right pocket.

ii) Eating his last chocolate cookie though it was not Gran, it was her cat Barry, and even though Mom says it is **CAT FOOD AND CAT FOOD ONLY**.

3. Digging up
George and Mildred,
who are a dead rabbit and
a dead guinea pig, which was
not completely my fault, it
was because I was being an
archaeologist and I thought they
were a baby two-headed dinosaur.

And Mrs. Butterworth says
no she cannot babysit because
she is still getting the sticky
stuff out from last time. And
nor can Mrs. Nugent and nor
can Aunt Deedee, who says she
would rather **PERISH**.

Daisy says she would rather **PERISH** than have a babysitter anyway, and we do not need one because she is eleven and big enough to babysit **ALL BY HERSELF** and she will be in charge of me and I will be on my **BEST BEHAVIOR**, you will see.

Only I do not want to see because I am not **INTO** Daisy being **IN CHARGE** because she has already bossed me three times today, e.g.:

a) No you cannot be a rock star because you are too **SMALL** and your hair is **WEIRD**.

2. No you cannot have a lemon drop because you are too **SMALL** and you have socks on your ears, which is **WEIRD**.

3. No you cannot borrow my old doll that does wee-wees because you are too **SMALL** and last time you made her drink red ink, which is **WEIRD**.

So I say I would rather **PERISH** than have Daisy as a babysitter. And luckily so would Mom, because she says she will call her friend Janice Ham to see who she uses and cross her fingers that she is free **TONIGHT**.

Only Janice Ham uses
Shaniqua Reynolds from the hair
salon, who is at a braiding
convention, so she says to call
Felicity Minky.

Only Felicity Minky
says she uses Kimberley
Puttock, who has a sore
finger, so she says to call
Alexis Boreham-Best.

Only Alexis Boreham-Best
says she uses Cosmo's mom
Sunflower, who is doing a
moon dance, so she says

she will ask Cosmo's cousin Hilary, who is training to be a nanny, so it will be better than **PERFECT**. And Mom is not so sure because she does not think anything that involves Sunflower is **BETTER THAN PERFECT**, but as Gran says, **BEGGARS CAN'T BE CHOOSERS**, so it is Hilary who will be here at seven o'clock sharp.

★ ☆ ✦ ✦

And so at 6:59 we are on **TENTERHOOKS** to see what Hilary will be like.

I say she is probably wearing a rainbow dress and will make us praise the sun and write poems about pixies.

Daisy says she is probably pierced on her nose and has purple hair and will not say a word except "Shut up and go to bed."

And Mom says she is probably **NUTS** if she has agreed to come and babysit us two, but as long as she does not eat all the cheese or blow the house to **SMITHEREENS**, then she does not care if she has purple hair or a pierced nose or makes us writes poems about pixies or elves or even Maximum Terror.

And before I can say it is Maxi*mus* Terror the doorbell rings. And I say,

Hurray, it is Hilary.

Which it is. Only Hilary does not have purple hair or a pierced nose or a rainbow dress, or even a dress at all. Hilary has orangish hair, and a T-shirt that says *Save the Whales*, and a beard – because Hilary is a **BOY**. Which is completely **UNPREDICTABLE** and Mom says so.

Hilary Who Is A Boy says,

It's a common mistake, but do not worry, I am almost completely qualified, and now it is time to shoo.

And I can tell Mom is about to say something about the shooing, or possibly about the T-shirt, but Dad says if they do not leave this **INSTANT**, Mr. Hobnob will do definite **FROWNING**, and Gran says if she doesn't leave this **INSTANT**, Arthur Peason will do definite **FROWNING**, so in comes Hilary Who Is A Boy and out shoos Mom and Dad and Gran.

And I am **INTERESTED** in Hilary Who Is
A Boy because I have never had a boy babysitter
before. And Daisy is also **INTERESTED** in Hilary
Who Is A Boy because she has scooted upstairs
and come back down in a completely different
dress and Rambling Rose lipstick, which she is
not supposed to wear except at a school dance
and I tell her so.

But she says,

Shut up.

And I say,

No, **YOU** shut up.

And she says,

No, **YOU** shut up!

And there is a lot of shut-upping until Hilary Who Is A Boy says,

Instead of **SHUT-UPPING** let's play rock-paper-scissors and whoever wins will be **SUPREME CHAMPION** and then it will be decided.

SAVE THE

Which is when me and Daisy **SHUT UP** almost immediately, because we are both very **INTO** rock-paper-scissors and also on being **SUPREME CHAMPIONS**.

But Hilary Who Is A Boy says before we are **READY TO COMMENCE** we must go to the kitchen, because playing rock-paper-scissors requires concentration and concentration requires **SNACKS**, which we are also **INTO**. And so we go completely quickly to the kitchen and we get **SNACKS**, which are:

a) Some carrots

2. A jar of sprinkles

3. A jar of honey

Because Hilary Who Is A Boy says the only way to eat carrots is dipped in honey and sprinkles, and for once me and Daisy agree. And so I say we are **READY TO COMMENCE**. But Hilary Who Is A Boy says in fact first we have to dress up as Hooligans because it is essential to dress as Hooligans when you are playing rock-paper-scissors and also eating carrots dipped in honey and sprinkles. And the good thing about Hooligans is that they wear whatever they like as long as it is using their **IMAGINATIONS**, and then we will definitely be **READY TO COMMENCE**. And so me and Daisy and Hilary Who Is A Boy go upstairs and use our **IMAGINATIONS**.

And I **IMAGINE** a Hooligan who wears a shower curtain as a cape and a wastepaper bin on my head (with the trash still in it).

And Hilary Who Is a Boy **IMAGINES** a Hooligan who wears a pair of Gran's tights over his head and a swim suit.

And Daisy **IMAGINES** a Hooligan who wears a pair of very tall heels and Mom's fake diamond necklace (which I know is fake because real diamonds do not crack if you bite them and I tested one once and it cracked and rolled under the dresser).

And then Hilary Who Is A Boy says we are all excellent Hooligans and so we are **READY TO COMMENCE** and so we do.

And to **COMMENCE** the **COMMENCING** we eat our snacks, and Hilary is right because honey and sprinkles is the best way to eat carrots ever and even I do not complain and in fact then I have a **BRILLIANT IDEA™** which is to test out other things to see if they are nice dipped in honey and sprinkles, e.g.:

1. A chocolate truffle, which is nice.

b) A pink wafer cookie, which is nice.

3. A string cheese, which is not nice, and even Barry agrees.

And then next it is time to play rock-paper-scissors to decide who is **SUPREME CHAMPION**. And at first I am winning because I do scissors, and Daisy does paper, and so I cut her and I win.

And then Hilary Who Is A Boy does scissors, and I do rock, and so I blunt him and I win.

But then something else **UNPREDICTABLE** happens, which is that next time Daisy does paper, but Hilary Who Is A Boy does **MAGIC FINGER**, which is wiggling it in a circle, and so he has won. Only Daisy says **MAGIC FINGER** is not real so in fact she should have won, it is the rules (because Daisy is very big on rules).

But Hilary Who
Is A Boy says
**MAGIC
FINGER** *is* real
and so is **FOOT
OF DOOM**,
which is
stamping very
hard on the
floor, and so is
**MYSTERIOUS
MONKEY
HANDS**, which
is waving them
around your
head like **CRAZY**.

39

And Daisy thinks in fact she really likes
MAGIC FINGER and **FOOT OF DOOM** and
MYSTERIOUS MONKEY HANDS and so do I,
and so we decide they are real and we can use
them from now on, it is the rules.

And then Daisy wins the next round because she does **FOOT OF DOOM** and Hilary Who Is A Boy does **MAGIC FINGER** and so he is stamped on.

But the next round Daisy does **MAGIC FINGER** and I do **MYSTERIOUS MONKEY HANDS** and so I have won.

Only Daisy is not
happy about this
and pokes me with
her **MAGIC FINGER**.

And so I use my **MYSTERIOUS MONKEY HANDS**
to throw a string cheese dipped in honey and
sprinkles at her **MAGIC FINGER**.

Only it misses and
hits Hilary Who Is
A Boy on the nose

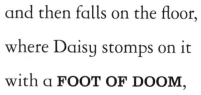

and then falls on the floor,
where Daisy stomps on it
with a **FOOT OF DOOM**,

which is wearing a very high heel and so it is quite **DOOMY**.

And I say, "Forsooth, you have **SMITED** my string cheese with your **FOOT OF DOOM** and so I will **SMITE** your necklace with my **MYSTERIOUS MONKEY HANDS**," which I do, because I am very **BIG** on **SMITING** things. Only it turns out that everyone else is also very **BIG** on **SMITING** things, e.g.:

i) Daisy says she will **SMITE** Hilary Who Is A Boy's Hooligan helmet of tights with a jar of honey, which she does.

2. Hilary Who Is A Boy says he will smite my Hooligan cloak with scissors, which are actual and not pretend ones from the game.

c) I say I will **SMITE** everything in the room with a jar of sprinkles, which I do.

Which is when something else **UNPREDICTABLE** happens, which is that Mom and Dad walk in.

And Daisy says,

Oops.

And Hilary
Who Is A
Boy says,

Ruh-oh.

And I say,

It wasn't me.

But Mom says it was, because wherever

there is a **HORRIBLE
HOOPLA**, there is
me in the middle of it.

45

But I say,

It is not **HOOPLA**, it is **HOOLIGANS** and also **FEET OF DOOM** and **MYSTERIOUS MONKEY HANDS**.

But Mom says she will be the judge of what is **HOOPLA** and what is not and she judges it **IS**, and frankly it is the last thing she needs after a night trying to do the American Smooth with Mr. Hobnob, who is neither.

I say, but on the plus side we have not eaten all the cheese and the house is not blown to **SMITHEREENS**, so in fact it is all alright.

But Mom does not agree and sends
Hilary O. Henderson home and sends me
and Daisy to bed without a snack, not even
a carrot dipped in honey.

Daisy says, "*It is all your fault, Penelope Jones, you are such a complete* **MORON**." But I say it is not my fault, it is the fault of Hilary Who Is A Boy.

And for once Mom agrees, because the next time something **UNPREDICTABLE** happens, i.e. the Operatic Extravaganza, she decides she and Dad will stay in after all.

Cosmo Moon Webster is my best friend

even though he is a week older than me and a boy because my mom says we are like **TWO PEAS IN A POD**, i.e. completely and exactly the same because we both like completely and exactly the same things, i.e.:

a) Pink wafer cookies.

2. Throwing e.g. erasers at Henry Potts, who is Cosmo's mortal enemy.

iii) Inventing a time machine out of a bus, some tinfoil and an alarm clock.

d) *Animal SOS,* which
is a program on TV where
animals almost
die and then they don't
and it is **MIRACULOUS**.

5. Digging for buried treasure, e.g. a
Roman coin and a mysterious key, which Mom
says is not mysterious, it is the spare key to the
back door which Dad buried in case we got
locked out, only when we **DID** get locked out
(which was not really my fault, I just wanted to
see if the key fit through the crack in the
pavement), he forgot where he had buried the
spare one so we had to
break in with a golf
club and a hammer.

But in fact we are not completely **PEA**-like because there is one big difference and that is that Cosmo is a vegetarian, i.e. he does not eat animals, not even one tiny bit of a chicken. This is because his mom Sunflower does not believe in eating anything that has been alive once, unless it is a carrot or a piece of broccoli or a squishy thing made of lentils, for instance. But I am **NOT** a vegetarian, because Mom says she is **UP TO HERE** with **PICKY EATING**, because Daisy, who is my sister and who is very irritating, is being doubly irritating because she says she cannot eat cabbage as it is **AGAINST HER RELIGION**, and so is asparagus and soup and fish (unless it is fish sticks and french fries). Dad says it is a very strange religion and Gran says it is a made-up religion and I say maybe I would like this religion because I am not **INTO** asparagus or soup either, but Mom says,

Oh for heaven's sake, it is **EAT WHAT YOU'RE GIVEN** and that is the end of it.

✦ ✧ ✦ ✦

Except it is not because the next day in assembly,

Mr. Schumann, who is our principal, and who is

normally saying things like "Penelope Jones, I

am **SICK** and **TIRED** of telling you that

corn is for swallowing, not pinging

at people," says something else,

and it is that from now on

there'll be Meat-Free

Monday, which

means e.g.

vegetable goulash

for lunch instead

of hot dogs.

MEAT-
FREE
MONDAY!

And almost immediately Cosmo jumps up
and says,

Hurray! It is a **VICTORY** for the animals!

But Mr. Schumann says it is not, it is a **VICTORY** for the school board who is in charge of school lunches, and not to get too carried away and also to please sit down because Cosmo's silver boots are distracting and it is time for Bridget Grimes (who is the star student of our class and Mr. Schumann's favorite) to play "A Bicycle Built For Two" on the recorder.

Only when we get back to the classroom everyone is completely carried away with Meat-Free Monday, even Miss Patterson, because she says it is important to be interested in where food comes from, i.e. not the supermarket or the corner market but fields and trees and farms, and it is especially important to be a **FRIEND TO THE ANIMALS**.

And Cosmo says he is **ALWAYS** a **FRIEND TO THE ANIMALS** because of being a vegetarian

and also because he once helped a worm out of a puddle with a ruler.

And then everyone is arguing like **CRAZY** about who is the best

FRIEND TO THE ANIMALS, i.e.:

1. Alexander Pringle (who wears age 14 sized clothes even though he is nine because he is mostly eating sandwiches when he should not be eating sandwiches) says he once rescued a fly that was about to be eaten by a spider, so **HE** is the best **FRIEND TO THE ANIMALS**.

b) Bridget Grimes

says she once rescued a
spider that was about
to be eaten by a cat, so
SHE is the best **FRIEND
TO THE ANIMALS**.

3. Cherry Scarpelli (who is
Bridget Grimes's best friend, and who I have
seen eat a crayon) says she has rescued a cat

from the animal shelter
and her name is
Tallulah, so
SHE is the best
**FRIEND TO
THE ANIMALS**.

iv) Henry Potts says he has rescued a **DOG** from the animal shelter and his name is Minimus Mayhem, so **HE** is the best **FRIEND TO THE ANIMALS**.

e) Cosmo says he has rescued a **MONKEY** from the animal shelter and his name is Henry Potts, so **HE** is the best **FRIEND TO THE ANIMALS**.

Which is when Miss Patterson says it is nice that we are all so **INSPIRED**, but that is quite enough being **FRIENDS TO THE ANIMALS** for one day and it is time to open up our math books instead and work out how many miles a car goes if it drives for ten minutes and is going thirty miles an hour and no it does not go around a traffic circle seventeen times.

★ ☆ ✹ ✦

But on the way home I have a

BRILLIANT IDEA™

which is that I am going to be the best **FRIEND TO THE ANIMALS EVER** and that maybe I can go to the animal home tomorrow and rescue e.g. a rabbit or a chicken or even an otter. Only when I get home Mom says **UNDER NO CIRCUMSTANCES** am I getting another animal, not even a **FISH**, because if

I get a pet then Daisy will want a pet, i.e. a pony because Lucy B. Finnegan has one, and Mom is already **UP TO HERE** with Barry, who is Gran's cat and who has just eaten four goldfish crackers and something with sticky stuff on it even though Mom says it is **CAT FOOD AND CAT FOOD ONLY**. Only I say,

But it is especially **IMPORTANT** because I want to be a **FRIEND TO THE ANIMALS**.

So Mom says if I am so **INTERESTED** in being a **FRIEND TO THE ANIMALS** I can start with Barry, because the sticky stuff has stuck him to the purple cushion and he is not at all **PLEASED** and nor is she because the noise is **INFERNAL**.

And so I unstick Barry, who is **PLEASED** again because he is not dragging a cushion around the floor, which is **GOOD DEED** number 1.

And all weekend I am doing more **GOOD DEEDS** to animals, i.e.:

1. I take Shaniqua Reynolds's dog Lennox for a walk to the salon and I only lose him two times.

b) I only eat two sausages at dinner instead of three.

c) I give the spare sausage to Barry, who is **PLEASED AS PUNCH**.

4. I do not stomp on a wasp that is sitting on the patio  looking like it might want to sting me at **ANY MINUTE** (only it does not, it wanders off toward Mrs. Nugent across the street, who hits it with a newspaper).

e) I collect fourteen beetles that are in the sandbox looking sad and give them a new home in a shoebox with some grass and some polystyrene peanuts and a sofa made of a matchbox.

And Dad says my beetle house
is a palace **FIT FOR A KING** and in
fact he could have been a zookeeper
if he hadn't met Mom, because he has
a **WAY** with animals. Only Mom says he does
not because he is scared of even a small snake,
plus the last time we went to the zoo
a monkey hit him on the hand. Only Dad
says that was not **HIS** fault, it was because
he was trying to rescue his sock. And I say
well that was not **MY** fault, it was because the

monkey looked shivery.

And anyway I do not
care, because I think I am
definitely the best **FRIEND**

TO THE ANIMALS EVER

and I will take the shoebox palace and the beetles in to show Miss Patterson on Meat-Free Monday and she will send me to Mr. Schumann for a gold star, and maybe I will even get to meet Griff Hunt who is on *Animal SOS* because my beetles have **MIRACULOUSLY** not died.

✦ ✦ ✦ ✦

Only when I get to school on Monday, Miss Patterson says in fact it is wrong to keep bugs **COOPED UP**, even inside a shoebox palace, because they are meant to be **FREE** and roaming the **WILD** and it is

indeed **MIRACULOUS** that they are still alive.
Only Henry Potts says they are not **ALL** alive
because, look, one is on his back. So I say he is
just taking a **NAP** because he is very tired from
the **ARDUOUS JOURNEY** to school. Only Henry
Potts pokes him and he is definitely dead after
all. And so Miss Patterson says at break I must
go completely quickly to the Nature Garden
and put the thirteen beetles who are not dead on
the compost pile.

And so at break me and Cosmo take the shoebox palace to the Nature Garden and I say, "Farewell, *it is time for you to run* **FREE** *and roam the* **WILD**," which is the compost heap i.e. some carrot peel and a

potato with a green sprout. And the beetles
absolutely do **RUN**, except for one who has a
leg stuck in the sofa, and so I rescue him **AND**
set him free and so I am even more of a
FRIEND TO THE ANIMALS.

Which is when I have my next

BRILLIANT IDEA™,

which is to set lots more bugs, or even bigger beasts **FREE** to roam the **WILD**, and Cosmo agrees and so off we go to find some.

And we have only gone maybe four steps when we find a creature and it is Marlon, the school goat, who is inside a special fence made by Mr. Eggs (who is our janitor and who smells like dogs), otherwise he eats a lot of things he should not be eating (Marlon not Mr. Eggs) e.g.:

a) Cosmo's orange.

2. Alexander Pringle's sandwich.

iii) Alexander Pringle.

But I say it is not very **FRIENDLY** that
Marlon is **COOPED UP** inside the special fence,
and Cosmo agrees, because his mom Sunflower is
very **INTO** animal rights and Cosmo says this is
almost definitely an **ANIMAL WRONG** and so we
must **RELEASE** him at once.

And so I unlatch the gate and am just wondering where a good **WILD** area is for Marlon to roam, e.g. our backyard, when Mr. Schumann shouts very loudly,

Penelope Jones, will you step **AWAY** from the goat enclosure, that is the fifth time this year.

And so I do step away and then I have to step straight back to our class, and for the rest of the morning I do not even think about releasing any more beasts because I am too busy racking my head to think of facts about Queen Victoria.

Only just as I am thinking about whether in fact Queen Victoria would have had roller skates, because it would be quite tricky skating in a long dress (and I know this because I have tried roller skating in Mom's nightie and now the skates are in the **OFF LIMITS** cabinet and the nightie is in the recycling bin), something **STRANGE** happens, which is that the light in the locust tank goes off and so do all the computers and so does the vacuum cleaner which Mr. Eggs is using to clean up the polystyrene peanuts from the shoebox palace.

And almost immediately everyone is "OOH"ing and "AAH"ing and wondering who has taken away the electricity, and Henry Potts says it is most possibly Minimus Mayhem, leader of the Herobots, who is going to use it to **DOMINATE THE WORLD** (because he is very **BIG** on Minimus Mayhem and on dominating the world). But Cosmo says it is most possibly Maximus Terror, leader of the Zombiebots, who is going to use it to dominate Minimus Mayhem and also Henry Potts.

But Miss Patterson says it is more probably a **GLITCH** or a **GREMLIN** and to stop **SPECULATING** and start washing our hands, because it is time for meat-free lunch and it is vegetarian sausages for us.

Only when we get to the cafeteria with our clean hands, another **STRANGE** thing happens, which is that Mrs. Feast 1 (who is the lunch lady and who once wore slippers to school) says the vegetarian sausages have gone mysteriously **MISSING**, and so it is macaroni and cheese and it is a good thing she boiled the macaroni before the electricity went out or it would be just some cheese, which is against school board rules (because she is very **BIG** on school board rules).

And so then we are all guessing like **CRAZY** who has taken the sausages, i.e.:

a) Mrs. Feast 2 (who is the other lunch lady and who is the sister-in-law of Mrs. Feast 1) says it is probably **THIEVES** or **VANDALS**.

2. I say it is a **GLITCH** or a **GREMLIN**.

3. Cosmo says no, it is definitely **MAXIMUS TERROR**, who is using the sausages to **DOMINATE** our school and we will all be zombies by recess.

Which is when Bridget Grimes starts to cry because she is not **INTO ZOMBIES** or **THIEVES** or **MACARONI AND CHEESE**. Only Mr. Schumann, who is not **BIG**

on school board rules or on Mrs. Feast 1 or 2 or on crying, says it is not **THIEVES** or **VANDALS** or **MAXIMUS TERROR** who have stolen the sausages, they are probably just **VICTIMS** of the **SYSTEM**, i.e. they are lost somewhere in the big refrigerator, and to sit down on our bottoms and eat our macaroni before it gets cold.

And so we are all sitting on our bottoms eating meat-free macaroni (except for Bridget Grimes, who is poking it with a fork, and Alexander Pringle, who is eating a sandwich) when something else **MYSTERIOUS** happens, which is that a noise starts coming from the

CONFISCATION CLOSET,

which is where

Mr. Schumann keeps

CONFISCATION
CLOSET

all the things that should not have come to school in the first place, e.g.:

a) Cherry Scarpelli's cell phone, which has seven different ringtones and one of them is "The Hokey-Pokey."

2. Jamal Malik's little brother Shoaib (only he did not go in the closet, he went in Mr. Schumann's office, although I think Mr. Schumann wishes it had been the closet because he broke the swivel chair).

Only the noise from the closet does not sound one bit like a cell phone or even Jamal Malik's brother Shoaib, because it is **MUCH** more **MYSTERIOUS** than that. And Luke Bruce, who can hang upside down by one leg from the jungle gym, says it is **JABBA THE HUTT**. But Henry Potts says it is not **JABBA THE HUTT**, it is a **WEREWOLF** who is actually Mrs. Butterworth from the general store because she has a mustache. And Cosmo says

it is not **JABBA THE HUTT** or a **WEREWOLF** that is actually Mrs. Butterworth, it is the **GHOST** of a **DEAD PRINCIPAL** (because he is very **BIG** on ghosts and also dead principals). Only Mr. Schumann (who is **NOT** big on dead principals) says it is not **JABBA THE HUTT** or a **WEREWOLF** or a **GHOST** because they are **NOT REAL**, and in fact there is probably a very **SIMPLE** explanation and he will open the door and **REVEAL** it.

And Mr. Schumann
is right, because when
he opens the door he
does not reveal
JABBA THE HUTT
or a **WEREWOLF**
who is actually Mrs.
Butterworth or a
GHOST, he reveals
Marlon, who is eating
a cell phone.

And then everyone is **DISCOMBOBULATED** and racking their brains to think how he could have gotten there, when I remember about unlatching Marlon's gate and Mr. Schumann telling me to step away. Which I tell Mr. Schumann, but for once he does not have time to be **SICK AND TIRED** because almost immediately there is

MAYHEM, because Marlon sees that
Bridget Grimes still has some macaroni
and cheese on her plate and he is very **BIG**
on macaroni and cheese so he runs
completely quickly to it, which makes
Bridget scream, which makes Marlon do a
goat noise and also do some poop that

looks like chocolate drops. And so everyone is saying "EWW!" except Henry Potts, who says,

Do not fear, Bridget, I will capture the dreaded Marlon and be a **HERO**!

(Because he is very **BIG** on being a **HERO**.)

Only Cosmo says, "Do not fear, Marlon, I will capture the dreaded Henry Potts and be a **HERO**." And so

Cosmo dives on Henry,

who dives on Bridget Grimes,

who dives into a plate of macaroni and cheese,

which scares Marlon,
who poops again and
runs out of the
cafeteria and down
the hall and onto the
playground,

which is where he
stays all afternoon
while Mr. Eggs
tries to catch
him with a net
and some
pieces of
macaroni.

★ ☆ ✶ ✺

So when I get home I am completely full of
GLOOM because I have lost three gold stars.

Daisy says,

It is all your
fault, Penelope Jones,
you are such a
complete **MORON**.

And Dad calls me Penny Dreadful and does
the honking goose laugh, but I do not see
the funny side because I was only trying to
be a **FRIEND TO THE ANIMALS** and now
Marlon will be locked behind the special
fence forever.

But for once I am wrong, because the next day Marlon has mysteriously **DISAPPEARED**, only he is not in the confiscated closet, he is on a farm with some sheep and a llama where he can be **FREE** and **ROAM THE WILD** and also not eat macaroni and cheese or vegetarian sausages or the fuse box.

And it was all Mr. Schumann's idea, so in fact it is he who is the best **FRIEND TO THE ANIMALS EVER**.

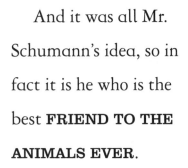

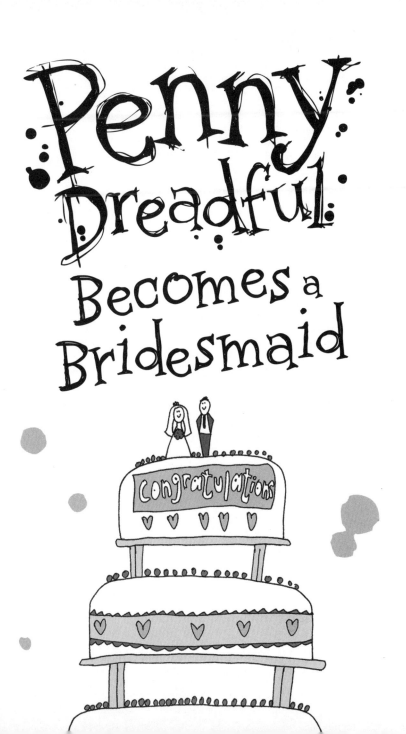

Daisy is my big sister,

and she is normally very irritating, e.g. when she is saying stuff like:

But at the moment she is doubly irritating because Lucy B. Finnegan, who is her best friend (except when they have had an argument about orange socks, for instance) is being a bridesmaid for the seventh time and Daisy has not even been a bridesmaid **ONCE**.

I say she is **CRAZY** because weddings are **FUSS** and **BOTHER** and I am never going to get married, not **EVEN** to Cosmo Moon Webster, not **EVEN** if he invents the first-ever time machine made out of a bus, some tinfoil and an alarm clock.

And Cosmo is not getting married either because his mom Sunflower does not believe in weddings, she believes in **FREEDOM** and **SELF EXPRESSION** and also **FAIRIES**.

But Daisy says in fact it is I who am **CRAZY** because weddings have **CAKE** and **KISSING**,

and she is very big on cake and especially kissing because she is going to marry George Helmet, who has the longest legs in Eighth Grade, and they will definitely kiss and have a cake and it will be three layers tall with white icing and real diamonds on it.

And Dad says,

Ooh, cake — did I ever tell you I could have been a baker if I hadn't married your mom. Maybe I will make a Swiss roll immediately.

But Mom says no he could not have been and no he will not because he burns even cookies and also she has had it **UP TO HERE**, what with Aunt Deedee calling fourteen times this morning only Mom cannot hear what she's saying because someone has superglued a pincushion onto the holes (which was not completely my fault, it was because Mom said she was **UP TO HERE** with Dr. Cement calling her about ear tubes and she was the one with an earache). Only now Mom will have to go over there to find out what the **HOOPLA** is, so could we please stop arguing about weddings and go and do something constructive instead.

And so we do and it is called betting, which Gran has taught us all about, and which we are very **BIG** on at the moment, e.g.:

a) I bet Daisy a jumping bean that is only a little broken that she cannot stand on her hands for seventeen seconds and she cannot so I win.

ii) Daisy bets me a sticker shaped like a tomato which has not completely lost its stick that I cannot hold my breath for seventeen minutes and I cannot so she wins.

3. Gran bets a dollar and a chocolate cookie that we cannot be **QUIET** and **STILL** for a whole episode of *Animal SOS* and Daisy can but I cannot so Gran half wins and so does Daisy but I am empty-handed.

But today Daisy bets me something super-special and it is her sparkly tights and I can have them if I can drink a glass of chocolate milk upside down without spilling any on the carpet. And I am very **BIG** on her special sparkly tights (because they make me look like Dr. Demonica, who is always freezing people with her evil heart of ice, only Magnificent Marvin melts her heart with his flamethrowing fingers, and so she is nice to everybody until the next episode) so I say,

Bet **ACCEPTED**.

And I drink the glass of chocolate milk, only most of it goes on the carpet and also on my shoes and so I do not get sparkly tights

but I do get tutted at by Dad, who says I will be in **BIG TROUBLE** when Mom gets home and it is lucky he is so good at **CLEANING** things and in fact he could have been a professional cleaner if he hadn't married Mom because he always gets things **SPARKLY** bright.

And so everything is all **SPARKLY**, except for my legs because of the no tights, which means I am completely unhappy. And that is why I have my first **BRILLIANT IDEA™**, which is to bet Daisy something she cannot possibly win and then I will get the tights for sure and so I say,

> I bet that you will not be a bridesmaid in the next three days and if I win I get the tights and if you win you get a year's supply of mint cookies.

Because I am not **BIG** on mint cookies but
Mom is always buying them. But Daisy says I
am **CRAZY** if I think that she will **ACCEPT**
that bet and she bets me the tights that I will
not be a bridesmaid in the next three weeks.
And so I say I bet her a horse named Horace
that she will not be a bridesmaid in the next
three years. And then she is just trying to
figure out what comes after three years when a
COINCIDENCE happens (which is not the same
as a **CONSPIRACY** because I have checked
with Mr. Schumann), which is that at that
very moment Mom comes back from Aunt
Deedee's and it turns out the **HOOPLA** is that
she is getting married to Mr. Bentley-Bucket
(who is not a vampire after all, which is

completely another story), and we are **BOTH**
going to be bridesmaids and so is Georgia
May Morton-Jones, who is my cousin and
who shows potential on the violin, and so is
someone named James Pants, only he is not a
bridesmaid, he is the **RING BEARER**. And so
Daisy is as **PLEASED AS PUNCH**.

But she says Aunt Deedee is **NUTS** for letting me be a bridesmaid.

And I say Aunt Deedee is **NUTS** for letting Daisy be a bridesmaid.

And Mom says the only person who is **NUTS** is Mr. Bentley-Bucket for marrying Aunt Deedee, who is mostly firing people for **NOT MEASURING UP**, so it will probably be all over before the wedding.

And I say when is the wedding and it is in three weeks so in fact we both win.

Only I do not g[...]

and Daisy does not [...]

cookies and no one g[...]

named Horace becaus[...]

both in **BIG TROUBLE**,

And so I [...]
then [...]

turns out Dad could not have been

a professional cleaner after all

because he forgot to make my

shoes sparkly bright and there are

chocolate footprints in the front

room and in the back room and

also on the bathroom wall (which

is not completely my fault, it is

because Daisy bet me I couldn't

walk up it like a fly and I cannot).

✳ ✳ ✳ ✳

...m completely **GLOOMY** because from
... on it is **WEDDINGS**, **WEDDINGS**,
WEDDINGS, which means on Saturday it is **NOT** going to Cosmo's house to see if there is a secret tunnel under the floorboards, it is going to see Mrs. Gutteridge to pick up my bridesmaid's dress which is made of white itchy stuff and no I may **NOT** wear it to school and pretend I am a ghost.

And the Saturday after that it is **NOT** going
to poke the dead pigeon behind the general store,
it is going to Hedges & Blunt to get a wedding
present, which is ten spoons (which is **NUTS** if you
ask me because who needs ten spoons at once, and
wouldn't a tortoise be better for instance, but Mom
says no it would not).

And the Saturday after that it is the **WEDDING**, which means **NO** doing lots of interesting stuff because I have to hold hands with James Pants and he will not want to be doing that if I have mud, or marshmallows, or anything frog-related on them.

Only I say I am not **BIG** on holding hands with James Pants because what if he smells like dogs, for instance (like Mr. Eggs, who is our janitor), and in fact I would rather **PERISH**. Only Mom says he will not smell like dogs if Aunt Deedee has anything to do with it, he will smell like soap and lots of it. And I say how much does she **BET** he will smell like soap and she says she is not a betting woman, but Dad says he is a betting woman (only not a woman) and he bets me a trip to Monkey Madness Safari Park that the wedding will be **FUN**, I will see. And Mom says she bets he will regret saying that, only I say she is not a betting woman so she is not allowed to say anything, which is when she looks like she is about to say something that **SHE** might regret. Only luckily Gran says,

Heavens to Betsy, is that the time?

And it is, and it is thirteen minutes past eleven and we were supposed to be at the church at eleven o'clock and so Aunt Deedee will be going **NUTS** and so will Mr. Bentley-Bucket and so will Reverend Bruton the pastor, who has to christen Brady O'Grady's little brother Anfield at one o'clock so there had better not be any **DILLY-DALLYING**.

And so we absolutely do not **DILLY-DALLY** but we get a bag of rice for throwing because it

is good luck, only our rice is mostly gone from the time I tried to see if it was true that pigeons exploded if they ate it and it is not, and so we have to get some very small pasta shaped like worms, but Mom says Aunt Deedee will be too **FILLED WITH HAPPINESS** to notice.

And then we rush right over to the church and there is Georgia May Morton-Jones with a basket full of pink petals and there is James Pants with a black shiny suit on and brown shiny hair and there is Aunt Deedee with a face like **THUNDER**. But luckily there is no time to be **CROSS**, which is not a **COINCIDENCE** but is **CONVENIENT**, because Aunt Deedee says,

It is left-right-left-right and no tripping anyone and no throwing rice until we get back outside, quick **MARCH**.

And we are quick-marching all the way up the aisle when James Pants says something very interesting, which is,

I bet you trip someone.

And I say,

I bet **YOU** trip someone.

And James Pants says,
"Bet **ACCEPTED**."
And so do I.
And so I am concentrating very hard on **NOT** tripping but

what happens is that I forget which is left-right and which is right-left and I get it wrong and I do trip someone and it is me, and James says, "I win." And I say, "Don't." And James Pants says, "Do." And Aunt Deedee says,

Shush.

But I do not mind the shushing because
I have had a

which is to do some betting with James Pants
because it is more interesting than the pastor,
i.e. Reverend Bruton, who is going on about
something to do with the bones of a man
named Adam. And so I am **RACKING MY**
BRAIN to think of a good bet and I think of
three and they are:

a) Who can invent a cloak of invisibility so
that we can hide in it and go outside and
dangle upside down from the oak tree?

b) Who can throw a piece of very-small-
pasta-shaped-like-a-worm the furthest (because

Aunt Deedee said no throwing of rice but she did **NOT** say no throwing of very-small-pasta-shaped-like-a-worm)?

3. Who can make Aunt Deedee scream?

And so I tell them all to James Pants and he says **BETS ACCEPTED**, only not number **a)** because we will also need a rabbit and a magic hat, and not number **3.** because what if Aunt Deedee screams so loud that Mr. Bentley-Bucket goes deaf and he cannot hear Reverend Bruton say "You are now husband and wife, etc." and so the wedding is **NULL AND VOID**, which means not happening. And so it is only one bet accepted really, and it is the throwing-a-very-small-piece-of-pasta-shaped-like-a-worm.

And so we are throwing the very-small-pieces-of-pasta-shaped-like-a-worm and I hit:

a) A tapestry of the Angel Gabriel

2. Some pink flowers on a table

3. Daisy's shoe

And James Pants hits:

1. A display of things made of raffia

2. A wooden eagle

c) Mrs. Dullforce, who plays the organ

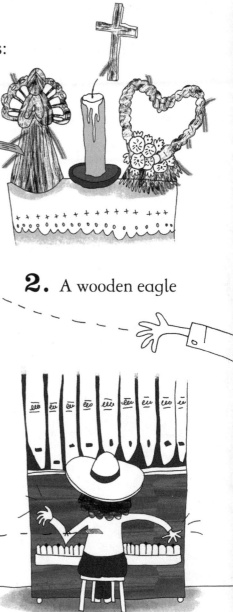

Which is definitely the furthest, so he wins bet number **b)**. But that is not all, because it also makes Mrs. Dullforce hit a note on the organ which makes Aunt Deedee scream, luckily not loud enough for Mr. Bentley-Bucket to go deaf, but loud enough for the best man, who is named Rolf, to let go of the wedding ring in fright, which pings through

the air and rolls onto the floor somewhere near Mrs. Butterworth from the general store. And so James is as **PLEASED AS PUNCH** because he is **SUPREME CHAMPION** of betting. But someone is not and that is Aunt Deedee because she says she needs the ring to get married or it will be **NULL AND VOID**.

And it is lucky Mrs. Butterworth has a beady eye because she finds it under Phoebe Patterson-Parry. And then the wedding is back on and there is kissing and everyone shouts hurray and throws rice, except me and James who shout "Yuck" and do not throw anything, not even small pieces of pasta shaped like worms, because Mrs. Butterworth's beady eye has also seen who threw the pasta and so it is confiscated.

But I do not mind because I have had my next ☼ **BRILLIANT IDEA™,** ☼ which is for bet number 4, which is who can find the best thing that is **BORROWED** and that is also **BLUE**, because it is very important to have four things at your wedding and they have to be one old, one new, one borrowed and one blue. And so Aunt Deedee is wearing Gran's sapphire necklace, which is old and borrowed and blue all at once, which is **CLEVER**, which is why she is a **BUSINESS GENIUS** and Dad deals with traffic cones.

And James Pants says **BET ACCEPTED** and we will do it at the reception which is at Aunt Deedee's house, which will make it especially tricky because of all the rules, e.g.:

1. No eating except at the table.

ii) No clay or paint or paste except at the table and only if it is covered in a plastic cloth.

c) No eating clay or paint or paste.

Plus if you even **LOOK** at a glass candlestick she says, "Do not even think about it, Penelope Jones."

And so when we get to Aunt Deedee's house I am definitely **NOT** looking at the glass candlesticks, not **EVEN** the blue ones, but what I **AM** looking at is a white cake that is three layers tall and on each layer is icing and not real diamonds but silver balls, and on the top it

also has a plastic man and a plastic woman
and a sign saying **CONGRATULATIONS** and
it is blue. Which is when I have my next
BRILLIANT IDEA™, which is that the sign
will be my thing that is borrowed and also blue
and it will be better than James Pants's thing,
and so I will be **SUPREME
CHAMPION** of betting after all.

So I am **SCOOTING** toward the cake
when Aunt Deedee appears in front
of me and says,

Do not even think about touching that cake, Penelope Jones.

And she says it has taken the Gilbey girls
seven hours to get the icing smooth and with no
bumps and in fact she will **MOVE** the cake out
of the way until the cake-cutting ceremony
because it will mean temptation is out of the
way too. And so she does and the cake is on top

of a cabinet in the kitchen where it can be **SEEN AND NOT TOUCHED** by any small hands. Which is true, because I cannot even touch the cabinet on my tippy toes, and I know this because once I threw a marble up there and I could not get it down for two hours until it rolled a little and fell on the head of Valeria Smirnov (who was the nanny before Katya Romanov, who was the nanny before Lilya Bobylev) and so Valeria had to lie down for an hour and forgot to make lunch and so Aunt Deedee fired her.

But Mr. Schumann, who is mostly saying that he is **SICK** and **TIRED** and it is mostly of me, is also saying something else and it is that we can do **ANYTHING** if we **PUT OUR MINDS TO IT**. And so I completely put my mind to it

and amazingly it works because my mind
thinks of an answer and it is: ○ ○ ○

If you pull that little table next to the
cabinet, and then put a chair on the table,
and another chair on the chair on the
table, then you will be able to reach the
sign which is the best thing borrowed and
blue, and you won't even have to touch
the icing on the cake, not one bit.

And so I do. I move the table next to the
cabinet and on top of that I put a chair and then I
realize if I just stretch a bit I won't need the other
chair, which is lucky because Mrs. Nugent is
sitting on it, and then I climb up the **AMAZING
TOWER** and I am teetering a little this way and a

little that way but I am **NOT** falling off **OR** touching the icing at all. And I am **JUST** stretching up to get the sign which is borrowed and blue when a **COINCIDENCE** happens, which is that Aunt Deedee comes into the kitchen and sees me and says in a very shouty voice,

What are you **DOING**, Penelope Jones?

So if you think about it, it is all her fault for being so loud. Because what happens is, I am so **SURPRISED** at the shouty voice that I do a little wobble, which makes the

AMAZING TOWER do a little wobble, which makes me do a bigger wobble right into the cake in three layers,

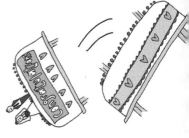

which does an even **BIGGER** wobble, and in fact it is so big it wobbles off the cabinet and onto the head of Dad who has come in to get some punch.

And then quite a lot of other things happen
and it mostly involves more shouty voices and
they are mostly at me. And Dad calls me
Penny Dreadful and does the honking goose
laugh, which makes cake fly out of his mouth

and hit Aunt Deedee on the nose, who does an even shoutier voice and tells us it is high time we all went home.

★ ☆ ✦ ✹

When we get home Mom is completely upset and says it is definitely the last wedding she's going to because they are too much **FUSS** and **BOTHER** and amazingly Daisy agrees.

But I do **NOT**, because in my hand is the blue sign after all, which means I win the bet because James Pants only got a sock that is Dr. Cement's, and so I am the **SUPREME CHAMPION** of betting and the wedding is **FUN** after all. And **THAT** means I also win a trip to Monkey Madness Safari Park, which Dad completely regrets because this time the monkeys steal his watch (which was not completely my fault, I was just seeing if they could tell the time) and so Mom wins her bet too, even though she is not a betting woman.

And I say I think I might get married after all and it will be to James Pants and I bet Mom a blue **CONGRATULATIONS** sign and a badge that says *I'm as bananas as a monkey* that it will be **FUN**.

Joanna Nadin

wrote this book –
and lots of others
like it. She is small,
funny, clever,
sneaky and musical.

Before she became a writer, she wanted to be a
champion ballroom dancer or a jockey, but she
was actually a lifeguard at a swimming pool,
a radio newsreader, a cleaner in an old people's
home, and a juggler. She likes peanut butter on
toast for breakfast, and jam on toast for dessert.
Her perfect day would involve baking, surfing,
sitting in cafes in Paris, and playing
with her daughter – who reminds her
a lot of Penny Dreadful…

Jess Mikhail

illustrated this book.
She loves creating funny
characters with bright
colors and fancy

patterns to make people smile.

Her favorite place is her tiny home, where she
lives with her tiny dog and spends lots of time
drawing, scanning, scribbling, printing, stamping,
and sometimes using her scary computer.

She loves to rummage through a good charity shop

to find weird and wonderful things.

A perfect day for her would have to
involve a sunny beach and large
amounts of spicy food and ice cream
(not together).

For Menace 2,
who is an excellent causer of hoopla,
but an utter inspiration.

First published in the UK in 2013 by Usborne Publishing Ltd., Usborne House,
83-85 Saffron Hill, London EC1N 8RT, England. www.usborne.com

Copyright © Joanna Nadin, 2013
Illustrations copyright © Usborne Publishing Ltd., 2013

A CIP catalogue record for this book is available from the British Library.

First published in America in 2016 AE.

PB ISBN 9780794535230
ALB ISBN 9781601303691
JFMAMJJA OND/16 02845/8
Printed in China.